Bullying: It Hurts

It's time to stop bullying!

Written and illustrated by
Brenda E. Koch

Hi, I'm Justice. I am seven years old and these are my friends.

I have FRECKLES, BROWN hair, and I wear glasses FOR Reading.

I Like eating pizza and playing video games.

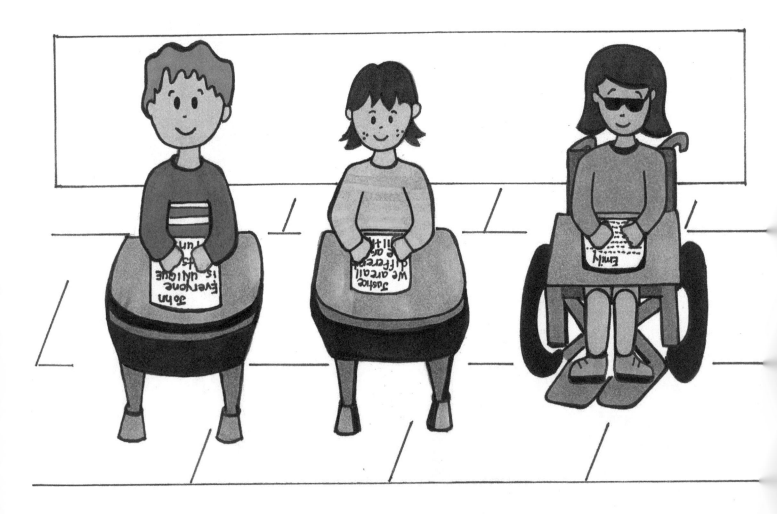

I Like going To school.

I don't like when people are mean to me.

Please don't push me.

Please don't throw
things at me.

Please don't hit or kick me.

IT HURTS!

Please don't Laugh at me or ignore me.

PLEASE
DON'T
DON'T
DON'T

STOP

IT HURTS!

I'M NOT GOING TO TAKE
IT ANYMORE!

Do you know what I am going to do about it? I am going to tell!

I am telling my mom, dad, grandma, and grandpa.

I am telling my teachers.

I am telling the police.

I am telling anyone who will listen.

Everyone will know you are a

BULLY!

About the Author

Before she was a grown-up and an advocate for victims of bullying, Brenda E. Koch was a bullying victim. In the years since, she has sought to improve the scene for children who might suffer a similar fate.

Koch has worked with kids—the bullies, the bullied, and everyone in these circles—for more than thirty-five years. With Bullying: It Hurts, Brenda is keen to eradicate bullying by empowering victims with the conviction that there are ways to successfully de-escalate potentially explosive scenes. They can be assertive, demand different behaviour, talk about what's happening with anyone who will listen. There is no call for these children to ever live with this in silence.

Koch has written two other books—LET'S PLAY and LET'S GO—for each of which she's won a Purple Dragonfly Award. She lives in Welland, Ontario, with her family and dog, Kilo. Koch has been an active foster parent for the last fifteen years.

Liked This BOOK?
Check out Books 1 & 2

YOU'LL LOVE THEM!

Liana, Age 7

Zoe, Age 4

Myla, Age 7

Mackenzie

Zander, Age 7

Faith, Age 10

BULLYING RESOURCES
THAT MIGHT BE OF INTEREST

Chrysanthemum. By Kevin Henkes. Grades: Preschool-3.

The Recess Queen. By Alexis O'Neill, illustrated by Laura Huliska-Beith. Grades: Preschool-3.

The Juice Box Bully. By Bob Sornson and Maria Dismondy. Grades: Preschool-5

Enemy Pie. By Derek Munson. Grades: Preschool-7.

Each Kindness. By Jacqueline Woodson. Grades: Kindergarten-3

Wonder By R.J. Palacio. Grades: 4-6

I would like to say thank you to Bonnie Procter, for being super creative and designing all of the characters in my books. The children absolutely love them.

I'm sending out a huge thank you to Eva, my daughter-in-law for all the work she has done promoting my books and for her continued support. Love you!

 FriesenPress

Suite 300 - 990 Fort St
Victoria, BC, V8V 3K2
Canada

www.friesenpress.com

ISBN
978-1-5255-5838-2 (Hardcover)
978-1-5255-5839-9 (Paperback)
978-1-5255-5840-5 (eBook)

1. JUVENILE FICTION, SOCIAL ISSUES, EMOTIONS & FEELINGS

Distributed to the trade by The Ingram Book Company

CPSIA information can be obtained
at www.ICGtesting.com
Printed in the USA
LVHW070847171019
634317LV00001B/1/P

9 781525 558399